A STORY PARTY AT
GREEN HEDGES

by

Enid Blyton

Illustrated by
Grace Lodge

HODDER AND
STOUGHTON

FIRST PRINTED . . . . JULY 1949

MADE AND PRINTED IN GREAT BRITAIN FOR HODDER
AND STOUGHTON LIMITED, LONDON, BY C. TINLING
AND CO., LTD., LIVERPOOL, LONDON AND PRESCOT

CONTENTS

MY STORY PARTY

I'M going to give a story-party! I'm asking fourteen children, and one of them is *you*. Of course I know you can't *really* come, though I wish you could—but anyway I shall tell you all the stories I tell at my party.

I'm asking Michael, Joan, Jack, Jennifer and Elizabeth (who are twins), Peter, Mollie, Daisy, Pat, Kenneth, Anita, Susan, Robin—and you. That's fourteen of you.

This is the invitation card I am sending out. Will you please fill in your own name, then it will be your invitation.

Enid Blyton

IS GIVING A STORY-PARTY AT

GREEN HEDGES

This invitation is for

....

Please come if you can

Have you filled in your name?

Now, at my party I am going to let each of you ask for your own special story—you can choose what kind you like, and I will tell you your story. As there are fourteen of you, that will be fourteen stories. I think we had better have tea in the middle, so that will be seven stories before tea, and seven afterwards.

Now, good-bye till the day of the party.

THE DAY OF THE PARTY

THE day of the party is here at last. I've got everything ready for you all. I expect you would like to know what I've got.

Well, there are honey sandwiches and banana sandwiches. There are sandwiches with chocolate inside and some with sardine in. I don't know which you like, but I hope you like all of them.

Then I have some little chocolate buns with icing sugar on top, and some buns I have cut open and spread with strawberry jam. I have made some biscuits in the shape of little men. There is a very big jelly in green, and a smaller one in pink and yellow. They are both wobbling in their glass dishes.

Then there is a perfectly enormous cake, with cream and jam inside. It has white and pink icing on top and all round, and I have put little sugar roses in the middle, and cherries and tiny hundreds-and-thousands round and about.

It really looks very nice.

There is a little china rabbit beside each of our plates, and between his ears each rabbit carries a small card. Somebody's name is on each card.

You have a rabbit too, and he carries your name.

Now it is half-past three. Somebody is coming up the path to the door. It is Michael—and behind him are Jennifer and Elizabeth, the twins.

And now quite a crowd are running in at the gate—Susan, Robin, Mollie, Daisy, and Kenneth. Come along in, all of you, and take off your hats and coats!

Where's Joan? And Jack? Ah, here they are, bringing little Pat with them. Peter's behind them—and Anita, looking rather shy. *You're* not here yet! Hurry up, or you'll miss the first story!

Now all the hats and coats are off, and we are in the big playroom belonging to my own children. They are away at school, so they are not here today. Sit down where you like, so long as you are near enough to hear me. Who likes the fire? Pat does and Susan. All right, they can sit in the chairs near the fire.

Are we all ready? Well, we'll let the story-party begin! Now, who shall choose a story first? One of the girls, I think.

You, Susan—what kind of story would you like me to tell you?

Susan knows the story she wants! She has been thinking about it all the way here.

"Enid Blyton, I've got a little black doll at home," she says. "At least, he's not at home now—he's here! I brought him with me. *Do* you know a story about a little black doll like mine?   He's so sweet, and I like his black face, don't you?"

"Yes.   He's a dear little doll," I say.   "What is his name?"

"Sambo," says Susan.   "And I want the doll in the story to be called Sambo.   Do you know a story about a black doll called Sambo, Enid Blyton?"

"Yes.   I think I do," I say.   "Yes—and *his* name is Sambo too.   Now, are you listening? Then I'll tell you the story that Susan wants. It's called "The Little Black Doll.""

THE LITTLE BLACK DOLL

A Tale for Susan

ONCE upon a time, children, there was a little black doll called Sambo. He was quite black, with tight curly black hair, red lips, and a smile that showed his very white teeth.

When he came to the nursery none of the other toys liked him at all, and he felt sad. He soon knew that the toys didn't like him because they turned away from him, and hardly spoke a word.

"Why don't you like me, please tell me why?" he asked anxiously, for he very much wanted to be friendly.

"Well, you see, you're black," said the big teddy bear.

"Why shouldn't I be?" asked Sambo astonished. "The golliwog's black, too, but you like him."

"Golliwogs always *are* black," said the baby doll. "We wouldn't like them if they weren't. But dolls aren't supposed to be black. You look queer to us."

Sambo was sad. "Well, I can't do anything about that," he said. "I was made black, and I suppose I must always *be* black. It's most unlucky for me."

He thought he would try and make up for his blackness by being very unselfish and kind. So he wound up the clockwork mouse twenty times a night, when everyone else was tired of doing it. He sewed on a button for the golden-haired doll, and pricked himself badly. He cleaned the windows of the dolls' house, and he washed over the floor of the toy fort when the soldiers complained of its being dirty.

But it really didn't matter what he did—nobody seemed to like him any better. In fact, they began to order him about, and tell him to do this, that and the other in a way he didn't like at all.

"It's no good," thought Sambo in despair. "They don't like me, and they never will. I can't alter myself. I shall always be black. If they don't like me

because I am kind and
friendly, they never will
like me. I feel very sad.
I shall run away."

So one night he did
run away. He waited
till the toys were playing
happily together, and
then he climbed up to
the window-sill. The
window was open at the

bottom. Sambo slipped out, and climbed down the
creeper that grew up from the ground below.

It was very dark in the garden. Sambo felt
rather frightened. Then it began to rain heavily.
Sambo had never been out in the rain before, and
he was most astonished. He felt the big drops
hitting him, and he put up his hand to see what
they were.

"They are wet drops," he said to himself, in

surprise. "Wet drops
falling down on me.
Oh dear, somebody
must have turned on a
tap somewhere. I shall
be drowned. I think I
had better go back to
the nursery, and run
away another night."

He turned to go back
—but he had lost his

way. He wandered about the big tennis lawn for a long time, getting wetter and wetter. Then he stumbled over a worm-hole, and fell down bump! He twisted his ankle, and it hurt him.

"I can't walk any more," he groaned. "I must lie still till my leg feels better."

So there he lay, out on the grass, with the rain pouring down on him, harder and harder. He was very wet, and cold and sad.

After a while the toys in the nursery missed little Sambo. They looked round for him, but he wasn't there. Then the golliwog remembered seeing him climb up on to the window-sill.

"Do you know, I believe he must have run away!" said the golly.

"Why?" asked the mouse.

"Because we didn't like him," said the bear.

"He was really very kind," said the clockwork mouse. "He wound me up ever so many times when you all got tired of doing it for me."

"And he did clean the dolls' house windows very nicely," said the tiny dolls.

"Do you *really* think he's run away?" said the mouse, upset. "I wouldn't like that. After all, he couldn't help being black. We were getting used to him."

"I think I liked him, after all," said the bear. "He was so unselfish and kind. I thought I didn't like him because he was different from all the other dolls—but now I think I did like him."

"And I liked him, too," said the golden-haired doll. "He didn't even cry when he pricked himself with the needle he used to sew on my button."

"I'm going to find him," said the golly, suddenly. All the toys thought they would like to go too, so they climbed up to the window-sill and out into the garden.

It wasn't very long before they found little Sambo, lying in the rain on the big tennis lawn. They picked him up and helped him to hobble back home. He was very wet and very cold and he sneezed a lot.

"I ran away," he said. "I can't bear you not to like me. I can't help being black."

"We do like you," said the golly. "We like you very much. We were silly. You just come back and live with us again and see how much we like you."

Now when they were all back in the nursery the toys had a great shock. They looked at the little black doll—and he wasn't black any more! The rain had washed his face quite white. He did look queer.

B

"What's the matter?" asked Sambo, seeing that the toys were all staring at him. "A-tish-oo! Do tell me why you are staring."

"The rain has washed away your black. You are white now," said the bear.

"Oh good!" said Sambo, delighted. "Now perhaps you won't dislike me because I am black."

"But I want you to be black!" said the clockwork mouse, almost crying. "You don't look like Sambo any more. It was Black Sambo I liked. I want Black Sambo back again."

All the toys felt the same. It was funny. They stared at White Sambo, and longed for him to be black again, the little smiling black doll they had known so well.

"This is dreadful," said Sambo. "First I'm black and you don't like me. Then I get white, and you still don't like me. I am very unhappy."

"Listen," said the golly, suddenly. "There is some black ink in the ink-pot. Let me get a rag, Sambo, and dip it into the ink and rub your face with it. Then you'll be black again and we shall like you."

So the golliwog took a bit of rag from the paintbox, dipped it into the ink and rubbed Sambo's face with it. In a trice he was black again. His eyes shone, his teeth shone, and he smiled as he had always smiled.

The golly hugged him. The mouse wrapped his tail round his leg. The baby doll kissed him. The bear squeezed him. He was their own little black Sambo once more!

"Now do you like me again?" asked Sambo.

"We don't like you because you are black or because you are white," said the golly. "We like you because you are kind and friendly and good. You can be any colour you like. We don't really care. Don't you dare to run away again, or we shall be very unhappy."

"I shall never run away if you are my friends," said Sambo, happily. And he never did.

"Oh—I did like that story," says Susan. "It was just the kind I like. And Sambo listened too—he did really!"

"Yes, I saw him," says Pat. "Enid Blyton, can I have a turn now? Do let me. I know exactly the story I want."

"Shall we let Pat have a turn now?" I say, looking round at you all.

"Yes. She's the smallest," says Jack. "Go on, Pat—choose your story. What's it to be about?"

"I do so like rabbits," says Pat. "I've got some at home. And there's a little speckly one, who's rather naughty. I call him Bobtail. I'm sure he's rude to his big mother. Do you know a story about a rude little rabbit called Bobtail?"

"Yes. It just happens that I do," I say. "But it's not a very long one."

"I don't mind," says Pat. "I like short ones. I can only just read, you see, so I always choose short ones. You tell me about Bobtail, the rude rabbit!" "Well, are you all listening?" I say. And, of course, you all are! Nobody is going to miss a word of the story. "Now here is the tale of 'The Rude Little Rabbit.'"

The Rude Little Rabbit

A Tale for Pat

THERE was once a little speckled rabbit called Bobtail who was very rude. He called cheeky names out after anyone he met, and he always answered back when anyone scolded him.

"Hallo, pins and needles!" he would say to Prickles the hedgehog. Prickles always got very much annoyed when anyone called him that.

"I shall tell your mother," Prickles said.

"Tell my father and my mother, my brothers and my sisters, my grandmothers and my grandfathers, my great-grandmothers and my great-grandfathers!" Bobtail said.

"I suppose you think you're clever," said Prickles.

"I don't think it, I know it!" sang out Bobtail.

Then he saw the beautiful kingfisher fly down to the tree. The blue and green bird was dazzling to look at, but he hadn't much of a tail, which always made him feel a bit sad.

"Left your tail at home this morning?" asked Bobtail, popping his head out of a bush.

"If you were my child I'd spank you and put you to bed," said the kingfisher, annoyed.

"If I were your child I'd find you a new tail and stitch it on!" said Bobtail rudely.

But one day he was rude to the wrong person! He was rude to the Spotted Goblin, who lived in the hollow oak tree.

The Spotted Goblin had once dropped a pot of red paint, and it had splashed up and spotted him with red all over. As it was magic paint, he hadn't been able to wash it off, so he had to have the spots for always.

Bobtail saw him coming along, and he pulled his whiskers and thought of a joke. He knew that measles had spots, so he called out after the Goblin:

"Hallo, Measles! How are your spots?"

The Goblin turned round and glared. "If you dare to say that again I'll put a spell on your ears!" he said.

Bobtail didn't believe him. "Hallo, Measles, how are your spots?" he said again, and then rushed off to his hole at once.

"Kikky, rooni, billi-noona!" shouted the Goblin in an angry voice. It was a spell for rabbits' ears, but Bobtail didn't know it.

The spell worked. When Bobtail got to his hole and tried to flatten his ears down over his head, as all rabbits must do when they run under ground, Bobtail found that he couldn't put his ears down at

all! No, they just stayed upright. It was queer.

He tried to force his way into the hole. His mother saw him, and spoke to him sharply. "You've left your ears up. Put them down, silly child."

" I can't," said Bobtail, in dismay.

"Don't be stupid!" said his mother. "All rabbits can put their ears down."

But Bobtail couldn't. It wasn't a bit of good. His ears stayed straight up, and even when his mother tried to bend them down she couldn't. She only made Bobtail cry out with pain.

"Well, you can't come into the burrow unless you put your ears down," said his mother. "You'll wear them out. What have you been doing to get your ears like this?"

" I was rude to the Spotted Goblin," said Bobtail, looking ashamed. "I said: 'Hallo, Measles, how are the spots? ' "

"What! You were as rude as that!" cried his mother. "I'm ashamed of you. You deserve to have a spell put into your ears, you really do."

Well poor Bobtail had a bad time after that. You see, he couldn't dash into his hole with all the other rabbits when an enemy came along. Sometimes it was a sly fox, coming to get a young rabbit for dinner. Sometimes it was a dog hunting. Other times it was a farmer with a gun.

Bobtail dashed off into the bushes, but it was easy for foxes or dogs to smell him out. He ran and ran, and they ran after him. He only managed to escape by leaping into a hollow tree and staying there quite still whilst his enemies rushed past.

"This is dreadful," thought poor Bobtail. "What a life I shall lead with ears like this. I never knew before how important it is for a rabbit's ears to be able to flop over."

One day he saw the Spotted Goblin standing at the top of Steep Hill. Bobtail made his way humbly to him.

"Please, Spotted Goblin," he said. "I'm very sorry I was rude to you. Take the spell out of my ears. I'll never be rude to anyone again."

"I can't take the spell out," said the Goblin. "There's only one way of curing those long ears of yours—and that is to throw you from the top of the hill to the bottom!"

"Oh no, oh no!" cried Bobtail, wishing he had never gone near the Goblin. But the Spotted Goblin lunged out with his foot and gave Bobtail a hard kick.

He rolled down the hill, over and over, over and over, head and back and heels and ears and tail, over and over. His ears were bent and he squealed in pain. He lost two whiskers. He hurt his foot. He bruised his bobtail—and he certainly bent his ears back till they nearly broke!

He sat up, feeling very shaky, at the bottom of the hill. He felt himself all over to see if he was still there. Two young rabbits came out to look at him.

"Do you usually come down the hill like that?" they said.

"Now don't you be cheeky!" said Bobtail, and he turned to chase them. They went down their hole—and he followed them. Half-way down he stopped in delight.

"My ears are all right again! They bent themselves down when I went into the hole. Oh good— now they are cured!"

But it was a very painful cure, for Bobtail was so stiff and bruised for days after that he could hardly lollop in and out of his hole.

"I hope you're cured of your rudeness now," his mother said to him.

"Mother, I'm the very politest rabbit that ever was," said Bobtail.

"What a change!" said his mother. And it certainly was!

"Oh, *thank* you!" says Pat. "That's just the kind of story I wanted. And do you know what I am going to do, Enid Blyton? I'm going to tell it to Bobtail when I get home—and perhaps he'll stop being so naughty!"

We all laugh, and so does Pat. Robin edges a little nearer me. "What story are we going to have next?" he says. "Whose turn is it to choose? Don't let's waste time!"

That makes me laugh. "Well, you choose one then," I say. "I'm sure you've got an idea ready!"

"Yes, I have," says Robin. "And I'm sure everyone will like my idea. Can we have a story about a boy who forgets everything? I've got a cousin called Fred, and he's got a *dreadful* memory—he never remembers anything he's told to do—he can't even remember to post a letter!"

"Oooh, yes—let's have a story about Fred," says everyone. "A story about Fred's bad memory."

"No," I say, "we'll have a story about Fred's Forgettery! That will be better still. Now, let me think a moment—yes—I've thought of the story. Here it is!"

FRED'S FORGETTERY

A Tale for Robin

THERE was once a boy who had a very bad memory. He didn't even *try* to remember anything, which made things even worse!

"Fred, you haven't got a memory, you've only got a forgettery!" his mother said to him, many times. "Didn't I remind you three times to call at the shoemaker's for your shoes and *now* you haven't remembered!"

"Oh Mother, I quite forgot," said Fred.

"But did you *try* to remember?" asked his mother. "No, you didn't. Now you will have to wear your old shoes with your new suit when you go to see Granny. That really is a pity."

One day the circus came to Fred's town. It really was a marvellous one. It was Mr. Phillippino's, and there were elephants, a giraffe, monkeys, and the funniest clowns you ever saw.

Some of the children went, and

they really loved it. Fred wanted to go, but as he had really been very silly that week, his mother said no.

"You forgot to take your books to school yesterday, and lost a good mark for that," she said. "And on Monday you forgot I had asked you to stay at school to lunch and you came home, and made a great fuss because I was out and there was no one to get you your meal. And this very morning I asked you to call at the paper shop and bring me back my paper, and you didn't. No, you don't deserve a ticket for the circus. That forgettery of yours is playing all kinds of tricks this week!"

Now, on Thursday evening Fred had to go to a nearby friend's house to borrow a school book he had forgotten. As he came back with it he saw an old man hurrying to catch the post.

"The post has gone!" thought Fred. "I saw the postman collecting the letters as I came by. The old man has missed the post."

The man stopped by the pillar-box and looked at the post-times, as he held up the letter to the slit in the red box. Then he gave a cry of annoyance, for he saw that there was no collection until the next day. He had missed the last post.

"What a nuisance!" Fred heard him say. "Missed the post! Now the letter won't get there till Saturday morning if I post it. I'd better deliver it myself."

He stopped Fred as the boy came by. "Do you know where Rockland School is?" he asked. "Is it far?"

"Yes, a good way," said Fred. "It's my school. I go there every day. You go down there and turn to the left and . . ."

"Wait a minute, wait a minute—did you say *you* go to Rockland School?" asked the old man. "Well, I wonder if you'd mind taking this letter with you to-morrow morning, without fail, and giving it to the headmaster?"

"Oh yes, of course," said Fred, and he held out his hand for the note. "I can easily do that."

"Thanks very much," said the man. "Now don't forget, will you? You'll be sorry if you do!"

Fred didn't tell the old fellow what a forgettery he had! He took the note and put it into his pocket, quite meaning to give it to the headmaster the next morning.

He didn't think to himself, "Now I *must* remember this—I will carry it home in my hand, and put it on my dressing-table so that I shall see it to-morrow morning. Then if I carry it in my hand all the way to school, I simply won't be able to help remembering to deliver it!"

No—he didn't try to remind himself at all that he had something to do for somebody else. He just put it in his pocket—and forgot ALL about it.

He didn't once think of the letter that evening. He didn't think of it the next morning. He forgot all about it when he got to school and took off his coat. There was the letter, safe in his coat pocket, hanging up in the cloakroom, and nobody knew it was there!

Friday came and went. Saturday morning came. That was the very last day of the circus! Fred asked his mother again if he could go, but she shook her head.

"I should think not, Fred! Do you know you forgot to call in and ask how poor old Mrs. Jones was yesterday, and I reminded you six times at least. The poor old thing was very hurt because I didn't send to ask how she was. Certainly you can't have treats if you don't even *try* to remember something!"

Fred went out to

play with his friends. They went to peep in between the railings round the field where the circus camp was. It did look so exciting. The boys wished and wished they could see it.

"The tickets are expensive," said one boy. "Usually they are half-price for children, but this circus has done so well, and been so crowded every night, that there have been no half-price tickets. I think the circus-owner must be jolly mean!"

Saturday went and Sunday came. That day the circus moved off. Some of the boys watched it. It was fun to see the elephants move away, dragging caravans behind them. The clowns no longer looked like clowns, for they were dressed in ordinary old jerseys and trousers. The horses were not so beautiful without their waving plumes. All the same, it was exciting to watch, as the big procession slowly made its way out of the field.

Monday morning came. All the boys went back to school again, and gathered together in the big hall for prayers and roll-call. They were about to go to their classrooms when the headmaster stood up again. He had something to say.

"One moment, boys," he said. "I have something to tell you. I have had a letter, this morning,

from the owner of the circus that was here last week.
I will read it to you."

The boys stood still, listening. The head began
to read the letter.

"Dear Mr. Kenley,
"I was astonished not to see the boys of your
school at the circus on Saturday evening. I had
hoped that you would allow them all to come and
take the front seats, as I had offered them to you
free. I hope you got the invitation safely. I
gave it to one of your boys on Thursday evening
to deliver to you for me as I had missed the post.
He promised to do this.
"Yours faithfully,
"Phillippino."

The headmaster folded up the letter and looked
down from the platform at the surprised boys. They
were nudging one another and whispering.

"We could have gone—gone for nothing!"

"We could have had
the front seats! They're
the best!"

"Who took the note?
Why didn't he give it
to the head?"

"What a shame! The
circus has gone now
and we can't see it."

One boy stood with-
out saying a word, his

c

face as red as a beetroot. That boy was Fred! Of course—that old man by the letter-box was Phillippino, the owner of the circus—and he had given the invitation to Fred—and he had forgotten all about it.   It must be in his pocket still!

"I've robbed all the boys of the chance of seeing the circus for nothing!" thought Fred, with horror. "Oh, why didn't I *try* to remember?"

"Well, boys," said the headmaster, putting the letter into his pocket, "if Mr. Phillippino is right, one of you took the invitation from him, and forgot to deliver it.   Who was it?"

Fred was frightened to say it was he who had forgotten. The boys would be so angry. He stood there, saying nothing, his face still red.

"Come, come!" said the headmaster, impatiently. "No one is away today. It must have been one of you. It is bad enough to forget to deliver a letter, but it is a great deal worse not to be brave enough to own up to it. I've no doubt it was quite by accident that the note was not delivered to me, but please don't make matters worse by not owning up."

Fred was terribly ashamed of himself. Was he a coward as well as a careless forgetter? Yes, he was a coward—but he'd put a stop to *that!* He would own up.

He heard his own voice, rather shaky and small.

"Please, Mr. Kenley, sir, *I* got the note. I put it into my pocket, and forgot all about it. It's there still."

There was a silence. The boys glared at Fred in anger, and then began whispering, calling the boy all kinds of hard names because he had made them miss going to the circus.

"Fetch the note," said the Head. Fred went out and brought the letter back. The Head opened it and read it out loud.

"Dear Mr. Kenley,

"It is my custom, when my circus has done well during the week, to offer on the last Saturday of the show the front seats free to any school in district whose boys seem to me to be the best-

behaved.   I would be glad to welcome your lads
on Saturday evening, and will keep one hundred
of the front seats reserved for them.

"Yours faithfully,
"Phillippino."

"Well!" said the headmaster, folding up the note.
"I'm afraid Fred has spoilt the treat for you.   Fred,
will you kindly write an explanation and an apology
to Mr. Phillippino today.   Dismiss!"

Fred had a bad time that day.   Every boy was
disgusted, disappointed and angry.

"Can't you remember *any*thing?   You're not
stupid, just lazy!"

"It's all very well to forget things that only
concern yourself, but when you spoil something for
other people it's different!"

"Let's leave him out of games.   Who wants a boy
who can't even remember to deliver a note for an
old man!"

It was a tremendous shock for Fred.   He must
get rid of his forgettery!   He must remind himself
to remember things in all sorts of ways, even if it
was a nuisance.   He must tie knots in his handker-
chief, write out notes and stick them in his dressing-
table glass so that he could read them in the morning
and remember.   He must keep saying to himself,
"What did Mother tell me today?   What did Mr.
Kenley ask me to do?"

"I must get back my memory and lose my
forgettery," said Fred.   "Then perhaps the boys

will forget what I have
done, and forgive me.
It's so horrid having no
friends at school."

So he is trying hard,
but it's very difficult.
What's *your* memory
like? I do hope it's
not a forgettery like
Fred's!

"Oh, *thank* you, Enid Blyton, for my story," says Robin. "I'm going to tell it to my Cousin Fred. Do you mind?"

"Not a bit," I say. "Perhaps it will help him to get a memory and lose his forgettery. Poor Fred! I hope he will never do anything so dreadful as the Fred did in the story. Fancy making his class miss a circus!"

"Whose turn is it now?" says Anita. "I do hope it's mine. I know the story *I* want!"

"What is it?" says Michael.

"I want a story about a cat," says Anita.

"Any special kind of cat?" I ask.

"Well, have you ever seen a Manx cat—a cat without a tail?" says Anita. "My auntie has one. It's a nice cat and I like it—but it *does* look queer! Do you know a tale about a Manx cat?"

"No, I don't think I do," I say. "But I expect one will come into my head. Oh, yes—one has come already. It's called 'The Cat Without a Tail.' Are you all listening?"

The Cat without a Tail

A Tale for Anita

IN Cherry Road there were six houses side by side, and in every house there was either a dog or a cat or both.

There was Scamper the terrier, and Tiddles the tabby. There were Smut and Soot, two black cats so alike that hardly anyone knew the difference. There was Scottie the Scottie dog. There was Tinker the mongrel. He was just a mixture of a lot of dogs. And there was Ginger the cat, whose coat was the colour of marmalade.

Now one day a new cat came to the house whose garden backed on to the six houses in Cherry Road. At first the other cats, sitting on walls or fences, only just caught a peep, but they said she looked a nice little cat. They thought they would like to know her.

But the new little cat was shy and frightened. She didn't seem to want to make friends. She vanished indoors as soon as any other cat appeared, and as for dogs, she was really scared of them.

The dogs and cats of Cherry Road talked to one another about the new cat.

"She's grey," said Scamper the terrier.

"She's small," said Smut and Soot.

"She's got a very tiny mew," said Tiddles the tabby.

" Her eyes are green," said Scottie.

" She's the only animal in that house," said Ginger, the orange-coloured cat.

"I'd like to chase her," said Tinker the mongrel.

The cats turned to stare at him, looking down their noses scornfully.

"You *would!*" they said. "You have no manners. You are a common little mongrel."

"Mongrels should be seen and not heard," said the dogs. "In fact," said Scottie, "I think it's a pity they should even be seen, or smelt."

"You're always horrid to me," said poor Tinker. And so they were. He had tried to make friends with each one in turn, but they all turned their noses up at him. Smut and Soot were friends, of course. Tiddles and Scottie were firm friends too, and often slept in the same basket together. Ginger and Scamper were friends, though they did not live in the same house. Only Tinker had no friend.

The other cats and dogs thought he was a horrid, common little dog. He was a merry fellow, always wanting to play, and as sharp as could be. But none of the others would have anything to do with him at all. So poor Tinker had to run round and round after his own tail when he wanted a game, which was fun at first, but boring after a while because he couldn't help knowing that his tail grew on the end of himself.

Now, the very next day, the little new cat jumped up on to the sunny wall that divided her garden from the one at the back. All the other cats and dogs ran to speak to her—but as soon as she saw them, down she jumped and ran for the house as fast as she could.

But not before the animals had seen something very queer indeed.

"She hasn't got a tail!" said Tiddles, uncurling her beautiful grey one.

"I thought that too," said Scamper, wagging his.

"How very peculiar!" said Smut and Soot.

"Poor, poor thing—someone must have bitten it off," said Ginger.

"A dog must have chased her," said Scottie. "A dog that knew no better."

"Yes, and that dog must be Tinker," said Scamper at once. "Didn't he say he would like to chase the little new cat? Disgusting animal!

First he chases the poor creature, then he bites off her tail! I vote we don't speak to him any more."

"Not a word!" said Smut and Soot.

"I always did say he was a horrid, common little mongrel," said Tiddles. "So did we," said Smut and Soot.

Just then Tinker ran up, wagging his tail. "Woof," he said. "What do you think? The butcher's boy . . ."

Then he stared in astonishment—for all the cats and dogs put their noses into the air and walked off. Not one mew or bark could Tinker get out of them. He was puzzled and unhappy.

"What's the matter?" he barked. "What have I done now?"

"Don't you dare to bark to us!" yowled Tiddles. "We don't talk to dogs who chase little new cats and bite off their tails."

"I didn't. I didn't!" yelped Tinker. But nobody believed him.

"Fibber!" said Ginger, and hissed.

"Story-teller!" said Scamper, and wuffed. "Go away. We don't want to have any more to do with you."

Poor Tinker. He was very sad. He found that the cats and dogs really did mean what they said, and it wasn't a bit of good going to them and begging them to talk to him. So he kept away, and put his tail and ears down, feeling very unhappy.

One day he went to the bottom of the garden and lay down sadly, wishing his mistress would move, so that he might make a friend somewhere else. "Though I do believe no one will ever make friends with a funny-looking dog like me," thought Tinker. "My ears are too long. My legs are too short. My tail is too curly. I'm an ugly dog."

"What's the matter?" said a voice above him. "Why do you whine like that?"

Tinker looker up. He saw the little new cat sitting on the wall. He put his head down on his paws with a grunt.

"Don't talk to me," he said. "You are the cause of all my trouble."

"Why?" asked the little new cat.

"Because everyone says I have chased you and bitten off your tail," said Tinker, gloomily.

"Well, you didn't," said the little new cat, with a purr that sounded like a laugh.

"Who did?" asked Tinker. "Nobody," said the cat.

"Well, did you get it caught in a trap, then?" said Tinker.

"No. I never had one," said the little new

cat. "I'm a Manx cat, and Manx cats don't have long tails. I've just got a stump of a tail. Look. We never grow long ones."

Tinker looked. He was very surprised. "It's not very pretty to have no tail," he said.

"I suppose not," said the Manx cat. "I'm always afraid of being laughed at or jeered at. So, as soon as I see any other dog or cat coming I jump away and go into the house. But it's very lonely, being somebody queer. You can never make friends."

"I feel like that too," said Tinker. "You see, I'm only a mixture dog, a mongrel dog. I'm not a terrier or a spaniel or a bulldog—I'm a kind of mixture, and the others don't like me. Now they won't speak to me because they say I chased you and bit off your tail."

"How silly," said the Manx cat. "Do be friends with me. You are a bit ugly, but you've nice brown eyes and a lovely wag in your tail. My name is Shorty. What's yours?"

"Tinker," said Tinker, joyfully. "Come into my garden and play."

So Shorty jumped down and soon he and Tinker were having a marvellous game of Round and Round the Raspberry Canes. They made such a noise that all the other animals came to see what it was.

"Tinker is friends with the little new cat!" said Ginger. "I must say she looks a nice little thing, even though she's got no tail."

"Tinker can't have bitten it off," said Tiddles. "If he had, she wouldn't like him."

"I'd like to be friends with her," said Scamper, longing to join in the game.

"Sorry, Tinker, for saying things about you!"

"Well—you can play if you want to," said Tinker, who was very forgiving. But the Manx cat didn't want to play with anyone but Tinker. She jumped up on to the wall and fled away.

"She's a bit particular about her friends, is little Shorty!" said Tinker, with a twinkle in his brown eyes. "I'm rather particular too. I don't think I want anyone but Shorty."

He strolled off and the others looked after him. They badly wanted to make friends with him now that he didn't seem to want them!

And after that Tinker had a grand time! He and Shorty became fast friends—and when she wasn't there to have a game, he could play with any of the others.

"And be careful I don't bite off *your* tails!" he would bark to them. "Woooof! I'm after you!"

"Well, I *do* think that's a nice story," says Anita, when I have finished the tale. "I like that little dog called Tinker. I wish he belonged to me."

"Yes. I'd like him too," says Michael. "It's not tea-time yet, is it Enid Blyton? We've still got time for some more stories, haven't we?"

"Oh, yes," I say, looking at the clock. "You choose one, Michael."

"I'd like one about marbles," says Michael, taking some out of his pocket. "Look, I've got some beauties."

"Why, you said you wanted a story about birds' eggs, when we walked along together!" says Susan, in surprise. "That's what you said you were going to ask for."

"I know. But I think I'd rather have one about marbles now," says Michael.

"Perhaps Enid Blyton knows a story about both at once," says Pat. "Do you?"

"Well, I might," I say. "Let me think for a minute or two. Yes—I am thinking of a story that has both eggs *and* marbles in it! It's the story of twins—and I'll call it 'Eggs and Marbles,' to please Michael!"

EGGS and MARBLES

A Tale for Michael

JACK and Jim were twins and they did everything together. They went to school together, played Red Indians together, ran races together, played marbles, and went bird-nesting with one another.

Their mother didn't mind anything they did, except that she hated them to take the eggs out of the birds' nests.

"It makes the birds so sad," she said. "It is so unkind of you, Jack and Jim. You don't want the eggs. You don't collect them. You just find the nest, see the eggs, and take them. It isn't fair of you. Let the birds have them—they don't belong to you, they belong to the birds."

But Jack and Jim went on taking the eggs just the same. Their mother found the bright, blue eggs belonging to the hedge-sparrow on the mantelpiece of the boys' bedroom. She was sad, because she loved the neat little brown hedge-sparrows that came about the garden in the winter.

"If you keep taking the eggs, we shall soon have no birds," she said. "Now listen—I will give you some beautiful glass marbles, if you will promise me not to take any more eggs."

The boys loved playing marbles. They promised at once that they would take no more eggs. Their mother took them to a toy-shop and bought them eight of the loveliest marbles you can imagine. They were very large, made of glass, and inside the glass were patterns of blue, red and yellow, curving like snakes. Jack and Jim were really delighted.

"Oh, Mother! Aren't they simply beautiful!" said Jack. "The other children *will* think we are lucky to have these! They will be our very best marbles."

The two boys were very proud indeed of the wonderful marbles. They showed them to the other children, who tried to make the twins exchange them for sweets, chocolates or toys—but Jack and Jim wouldn't.

"No," said Jack. "They are the best marbles in the world. We shall never part with them.

We shall keep them till we are grown up, and even then we won't give them away."

The twins kept their word to their mother for a while, and did not take a single egg. Then, coming home from school one day, Jack saw a robin fly up from the ditch nearby.

"I bet there's a nest there," he said, and he began to look. Sure enough, there *was* a nest, made of moss and dead leaves. In the nest were three pretty red-brown eggs.

"Robin's eggs," said Jack. "Let's take them."

"We said we wouldn't," said Jim. "Look out— there's the robin come back. Hallo—it's angry!"

The little hen robin was indeed angry. The twins had robbed her first nest of her eggs, and her second one as well.

Now she had laid three more eggs in this nest, and she wanted to hatch them, and have the joy of seeing tiny nestlings cuddled in the cosy nest.

She flew right into Jack's face, and then flapped round Jim's head. The boys laughed. "Silly little thing! As if *you* could stop us taking your eggs! We'll take them just to spite you."

D

The two boys took the three little warm eggs from the nest. The robin was broken-hearted. She flew angrily round their heads, making such a noise that two big jackdaws, flying overhead, came down to see what the matter was.

They found the little robin sitting on the edge of her nest. Her heart was filled with sadness. Her third batch of eggs was gone. It wasn't any good laying any more. She would have no little ones to feed and love that summer.

The jackdaws listened to all she sang to them. "It's time we did something to stop those boys from robbing our nests," said the first jackdaw. "Do boys have eggs of their own? Shall we go and steal *their* eggs?"

The robin didn't know anything about boys, except that they stole eggs from her nest and from the nests of other birds. "I wish you *would* steal their eggs, if they have any," she sang, in her creamy voice. "I wish you would!"

The jackdaws flew off. They saw the house the boys went into. They flew down to the roof. Then they heard the voices of the boys in the bedroom below.

"We'd better hide these robin eggs ; Mother would be very upset if she saw them. After all, we did promise we wouldn't take any more."

The jackdaws waited until they could no longer hear voices, and then they flew down to the window-sill of the bedroom. No one was there. They flew into the room, and walked about the floor, looking for any eggs that might belong to the boys.

"Look!" said the first jackdaw, suddenly. "Eggs! Large, round eggs, all bright and shining."

The other jackdaw looked. In a box, arranged on cotton-wool, were the eight beautiful glass marbles belonging to the boys. The big birds had no idea they were playthings. To them they seemed like big round eggs.

"These are the eggs belonging to the two boys," clacked the first jackdaw. "See the nest of wool they are in! We will take all the eggs away. Then they will not hatch and the boys will know what it is to feel unhappy."

So, one by one, the jackdaws carried away the big glass marbles. They took them to their own enormous nest of sticks, high up in the church tower. There they put the eight wonderful marbles.

The twins came upstairs just as the jackdaws flew out of the window with the last two marbles in their beaks. They gave a scream.

"Our marbles! Mother, Mother, quick! The jackdaws have taken our marbles. They're all gone! Mother, Mother!"

Their mother came running in. She looked at the empty box.

"Poor Jack—poor Jim!" she said. "You know, jackdaws love bright, shiny things. They must have come along and seen your marbles, and taken them off. They once took a silver thimble of mine."

"No, Mother, no, they didn't take our marbles because they like shiny things," sobbed Jack, so upset that he couldn't help owning up to his mother. "We broke our promise to you—we took some robin eggs—there they are, look, in this drawer—and I'm sure the jackdaws have come along and taken our

marbles to punish us! We saw two flying overhead when we stole the robin eggs."

Mother looked shocked and sad. "To take eggs
is horrid—but to break your word to me when I
trusted you is dreadful," she said. "To think that
my own two little boys should do that, when they
love me and I love them!"

She didn't say any more. She went downstairs
by herself. The boys were dreadfully upset,
because they really did love their mother. They
rushed after her to comfort her.

"We'll never do it again!"

"You can trust us, you can really!"

"We're awfully sorry. Forgive us and give us
another chance, Mother. Don't look like that!"

"Of course I'll forgive you and give you another
chance," said their mother. "But I'm afraid you've
lost your marbles."

They had. They are in the nest of the jackdaws,
high up in the church tower—but they haven't
hatched yet!

Everyone stares at me as I finish the story. Michael looks rather solemn. "Do you suppose the twins will ever get back their marbles?" he says.

"Well, no, I don't," I say. "Do you think they deserve to?"

"No," says Michael. "But they did sound such nice marbles. I shan't let jackdaws get mine!"

There comes a clattering noise from the kitchen. "Oh, dear—is that somebody making the tea already?" says Joan. "Quick, Enid Blyton, begin another story!"

"Well, what is it to be?" I ask.

"I thought of rather a silly idea for a story," says Joan. "I don't expect you can make one up for it. You know, when I laugh a lot, I get a stitch in my side. It catches me just here. Could you possibly tell us a story about somebody who got a stitch, and what happened to it?"

"Of course she can't think of a story about a silly thing like a stitch," says Robin. "Can you, Enid Blyton?"

"Well, as it happens, I can," I say. "Aha! You haven't caught me out yet. Did you ever hear the story of Sally's stitch? You didn't? Very well, here it is."

SALLY'S STITCH

A Tale for Joan

SALLY was a little girl who was always laughing, so you can guess she was rather nice. I do like people who laugh, don't you? Well, you would have liked Sally very much. Everybody did.

One day she went for a walk across the fields. She went quietly, for the grass was thick and soft. And quite suddenly she came across five or six pixies playing the most surprising games. Sally knew they were pixies because she had seen pictures of them in books, just as you have. She was simply delighted. She sat down behind a bush and watched.

"I can stand on my head on the gate-post!" cried a small pixie—and he did. It was really funny to see him.

"I can curl myself up into a ball and roll along!" cried another. And he curled himself up, arms and legs and all, and began to roll over and over just like a ball. All the pixies laughed to see him.

"Can you bounce yourself, can you bounce yourself?" squealed a pixie nearby. "Oh, do try!"

"Of course I can!" cried the ball-pixie, and he threw himself up into the air. "Look out—I'm going to bounce!"

And he bounced. Goodness, how he bounced! Just as if he were a big rubber ball. Up into the air he went, and down he came again. He bounced on to a prickly thistle, gave a loud yell, and bounced high again.

Sally began to laugh. She couldn't help it. She laughed till the tears came into her eyes. Then she got a stitch in her side from laughing, and that made her feel very uncomfortable. "Oh dear," she said, "oh dear!" And she put her hand against her side to try and ease

the stitch there. You know how funny you feel
when you get a stitch in your side from running or
laughing, don't you?

The pixies heard Sally's laughter. It was a nice
sound. They ran round the bush to see who was
there. And they found Sally, laughing away, with
her hand pressed to her side.

"What's the matter?" they cried anxiously.
"Why do you hold yourself there? Are you hurt?"

"Oh, I've got such a big stitch in my side!" said
Sally. "I can't get rid of it. Oh, it hurts me! I
can't breathe properly. I can't walk with it,
either."

" Poor little girl!" cried a big pixie. "Who put
the stitch there? Did you sew it there yourself?
Was the needle sharp?"

"Of course not," said Sally, beginning to giggle
again. "Don't be so silly."

"Poor child!" said the pixies, looking at Sally out
of their funny green eyes. "She's got a stitch in her
side. Somebody has stitched her up so that she
can't walk properly. Poor child."

"Oh, don't make me laugh again or my stitch will get worse!" cried Sally. "Oh dear—it's the worst stitch I've ever had. But really, you did look so funny when you bounced on that thistle, pixie. Oh my—I shall start laughing again if I'm not careful!"

She tried to walk a few steps, but she couldn't because of the stitch in her side. The pixies felt really sorry for her. They talked among themselves.

"Let's call Dame Snippit. She can take out the stitch. The poor girl will never get home. What a shame that somebody has stitched her up like that."

"Dame Snippit! Dame Snippit!" called a pixie, loudly. "Are you anywhere about? You're wanted."

To Sally's enormous surprise, a neat little door opened in a nearby oak tree and out stepped a funny, plump old dame, with her hair in ringlets, and her waist all hung about with scissors and tape-measures.

"What's the matter?" she asked.

"This poor child has got a stitch in her side, so she can't walk," explained a pixie. "Can you take out the stitch?"

"I could snip it," said Dame Snippit, taking up her largest pair of scissors. "That's the quickest way of taking out a stitch, you know."

"Oh, I don't want it snipped," said Sally, in alarm. "It's not that kind of stitch, really it isn't."

"Well, what sort of a stitch is it then, my dear?" asked Dame Snippit, in surprise.

"Well—it's a laughing-stitch," said Sally.

"Never heard of one," said Dame Snippit. "Come, come—let me snip it for you, then you can walk. You shouldn't let people put a stitch in your side like that. Very silly of you."

"I didn't, I didn't," said Sally, and she tried to run away. But the stitch in her side caught her and she had to stop. She saw Dame Snippit take up her scissors again.

Then Sally remembered that her mother had always said she could get rid of a stitch in her side by bending over and touching her toes with her fingers.

"I'd better try that before Dame Snippit does anything stupid!" thought the little girl. So she bent herself right over and touched her toes. When she stood up straight again, lo and behold! her stitch was quite gone! Hurray!

"The stitch is gone!" she cried. "It's all right, pixies, it's all right, Dame Snippit. The stitch is gone."

"I suppose you broke it when you bent over," said Dame Snippit, in astonishment. "Well, well—don't you go having stitches inside you any more. Most uncomfortable, I call it."

Sally said good-bye and ran home. On the way she remembered again how the pixie had bounced

himself on the prickly thistle, and she stopped and began to laugh.

And she got another stitch in her side! But she didn't say a word about it. No—she wasn't going to have Dame Snippit trying to snip the stitch with her big scissors!

Do you ever get a stitch? Well, try Sally's way of curing it, and see if it goes!

"I liked that story," says Joan. "Thank you. I wish I had a stitch in my side this very minute—then I'd touch my toes and see if it went."

"Does it really go if you do that?" asks Michael, and he stands up solemnly, and bends over and back, over and back.

"It's no good doing it without a stitch, silly," said Joan. "How many stories have we had now?"

"Six," says Pat. "I've been counting. You said we could have seven before tea, and seven afterwards, Enid Blyton, didn't you?"

"Yes," I say. "So there's one more. Who will choose it?"

"Me, please," says Mollie. "And I want one with pixies and fairies in. I love that kind of story. And I'd like a *naughty* pixie, please."

"Oooh, yes—a naughty one," says Pat, scraping her chair a little nearer to me. "A *very* naughty one! Do you know one?"

"Oh, dear me, yes—I know plenty about the fairy folk," I say. "Now let me see—which shall I tell you? I'll tell you about Tickle the dishonest little pixie—and how he was cured of his bad ways. The story has a queer name —it's called 'What an Alarm!'"

WHAT AN ALARM!

A Tale for Mollie

IN the village of Tickle there lived a most dishonest little pixie. His name was Light-Fingers, and it was really astonishing the amount of things he took from other people without being seen.

He would take an apple from outside Dame Cherry's shop. He would take a biscuit from the tin in Mrs. Soap's store. He would pick flowers from old Dame Lucy's garden when she was out, and steal the pears from the big tree in Farmer Corn's orchard. And although everyone felt quite certain that it was Light-Fingers who was the thief, nobody ever managed to see him. He really was very clever.

"If only we could think of some way to catch him," said Farmer Corn.

"I don't like accusing anyone of stealing unless I actually see them doing wrong with my own eyes," said Dame Lucy.

"Quite right," said Dame Cherry. "We must never accuse anyone unless we can prove ourselves to be right. But dear me, how are we to prove ourselves right about naughty little Light-Fingers?"

Tick-Tock, the watch-maker, came up at that moment. He was a little bent old fellow with eyes as bright as a bird's.

"Hello, Tick-Tock," said Farmer Corn. "Now just you use your brains and help us. We want to catch Light-Fingers and punish him for stealing. But we don't know how to catch him, because he's so clever. Can you think of a way?"

"Yes," said Tick-Tock, after a moment. "I think I can. Light-Fingers comes by my shop every day on his way to and from the market. I'll put a clock on my window-sill and a notice on my door that says ' GONE OUT.' And if Light-Fingers doesn't take that clock I'll eat my best Sunday hat!"

"But if we hide behind a bush to watch, he's sure to know," said Farmer Corn. "He's so very, very smart. He wouldn't take it unless he felt quite certain he wouldn't be seen and wouldn't be found out either."

"Now listen," said Tick-Tock, with a smile. "That clock is going to be an *alarm*-clock—*you* know, the kind that goes off and rings a bell very loudly at a certain time. Well, I shall set the alarm for twelve o'clock, and it will go off then, just when Light-Fingers is marketing. That will give him a shock—especially when I come up and demand my clock!"

"Now that *is* a good idea!" said everyone, pleased. "We won't be anywhere about at all when Light-Fingers takes the clock ; but we'll ALL be in the market at twelve o'clock!"

So the next morning, when Light-Fingers passed by Tick-Tock's little shop, his sharp eyes saw a very fine green clock sitting by itself on the shop window-sill. Light-Fingers was surprised. Then he saw the notice on the door, "GONE OUT", and his sharp eyes gleamed. He took a quick look round.

"There's nobody about at all," he thought to himself. "Not a soul! This *is* a bit of luck! And I've got my old suit on, too, with its big pockets! Hurrah! I can put the clock in nicely, and nobody will guess it is there, for I'll put my big red hand-kerchief over it."

So in a trice the clock was in his pocket, with his red hanky draped over it. Then off to the market went Light-Fingers, whistling merrily. He thought he would be able to sell the clock for a lot of money when he went visiting in the next town.

The market seemed very full that morning. Light-Fingers was quite surprised. People seemed to be whispering together, and nudging one another. He wondered what it was all about. But nobody told him. Nobody whispered to him that an alarm-clock was going off at twelve o'clock that morning, and that he, Light-Fingers, was going to get a terrible shock!

At eleven o'clock the town crier went round the market, ringing his bell and shouting loudly:

"Lost or stolen! A beautiful green clock from

Tick-Tock's window-
sill! Lost or stolen! A
beautiful green clock
from Tick-Tock's win-
dow-sill! Please bring
to me at once if you
have it!''

"I haven't seen it!"
said Dame Lucy, and
she turned to Light-
Fingers. "Have *you?*"

"Dear me, no," said
naughty Light-Fingers,
untruthfully, "If I *had*
seen it, I would have
taken it back to poor Tick-Tock at once."

"I'm afraid someone must have stolen it," said
Tick-Tock, sadly. "Light-Fingers, what do you
think we ought to do to the thief, if we catch him?"

"Well, if anyone was horrid enough to steal your
clock, they ought to be very well punished indeed,"
said Light-Fingers. "I think the thief ought to
get one hard spank from everyone in the village.
If that didn't cure him, then what about taking
him to the Bad-Tempered Wizard? I'm sure *he*
would cure anyone in no time!"

"Good idea!" cried everyone. "A very good
idea. We agree with you, Light-Fingers."

Now, as twelve o'clock drew nearer, everyone
pressed close to Light-Fingers, eager to hear the
alarm clock go off. Light-Fingers couldn't imagine

E

why the crowds seemed to be everywhere around him. He couldn't seem to get away from them.

Then the market-clock struck twelve—and almost immediately afterwards the alarm clock went off loudly. My goodness, the noise it made! It had the loudest alarm of any clock in Tick-Tock's shop, and it made Light-Fingers almost jump out of his skin!

"R-r-r-r-r-ring! R-r-r-r-ring! R-r-r-r-ring!"

The alarm clock went off with a terrific noise. Everyone giggled. Light-Fingers jumped high into the air and clapped his hand to his pocket. Goodness! What could be happening?

"R-r-r-r-ring! R-r-r-r-ring!"

"What's that ringing? Where does the noise come from?" yelled Light-Fingers.

"It comes from your pocket," said Tick-Tock, with such a stern look on his face that Light-Fingers suddenly felt frightened. "WHAT have you got in your pocket?"

"N-n-n-n-nothing—except my red hanky," stammered Light Fingers.

"Hankies don't ring like that," said Tick-Tock.

"R-r-r-r-ring! R-r-r-r-ring!" went the alarm clock gaily. It seemed as if it would never stop!

"If you have nothing but your hanky in your

pocket, let me see what it is that is ringing," said Tick-Tock. "Have you a magic ringing spell?"

"No," said Light-Fingers. "And, anyway, I don't want you looking into my pockets. That's a nasty thing to do."

But before he could stop Tick-Tock, the watch-maker had put his small hand deep into Light-Fingers' pocket—and pulled out—his alarm clock, still gaily ringing for all it was worth.

"HO!" said Tick-Tock, in a terrible stern voice. "HO! So that is where my beautiful green alarm clock went—into your pocket—where many other things have gone, I've no doubt. Light-Fingers, you are a little thief, a nasty horrid little thief. I am glad you said what the punishment for a little thief should be. Let me see—what was it?"

Light-Fingers began to tremble. "I-I-d-d-don't remember," he stammered.

But everyone else remembered, of course. "Light-Fingers said one hard spank from everyone in the village!" a score of voices called out gleefully. Most of the people there had had things taken from them at sometime or other by Light-Fingers, so they were pleased to think they could give him one hard spank each. That would teach the bad pixie not to steal!

And so Light-Fingers got the punishment he himself suggested, and dear me, he didn't like it at all, especially when it was Farmer Corn's turn, because his hand was simply enormous and dreadfully hard.

Tick-Tock took his clock back home, and everyone giggled when they thought of the trick the clock had played on Light-Fingers.

"And remember, pixie, just remember what you said should happen to a thief who wasn't cured by Spanks," said the watchmaker solemnly. "You said he had better be sent to the Bad-Tempered Wizard. So BE CAREFUL!"

Light-Fingers *is* careful. He has been quite honest for a long time now, so perhaps he really is cured.

INTERVAL for TEA

"That's *just* the sort of story I like!" says Mollie. "I like people to be cured of things. Was Tickle ever sent to the Bad-Tempered Wizard, do you suppose?"

"I shouldn't think so," I say. "If I ever hear that he was, I'll let you know. That will be another story for you someday, perhaps. But now—what about TEA?"

"Yes! TEA!" shouts everyone, and they all take their chairs to the table in the other room. How their eyes gleam when they see the sandwiches and biscuits and buns and jellies and cake!

"Can we have a story while we have tea?" asks Anita.

"Good gracious, no!" I say. "Can't I have some tea too? You wouldn't like me to tell you stories with my mouth full, would you?"

"We wouldn't mind," says Mollie. "But perhaps it wouldn't be very nice for you. We'll let you off while you have tea!"

"That's very kind of you," I say. "Now who is going to pass the sandwiches? And who wants lemonade to drink? Pass your mugs, please."

Soon we are all having a very good tea. I look round the table—what a lot of children! But there is one empty chair—it's *yours!* Sit down in it quickly and join us. What kind of sandwich will you have?

Can you see your empty chair in the picture, waiting for you? Perhaps you can paste a photograph of yourself there, so that you are at the table too. I don't like you to be left out.

We eat all the sandwiches. We eat all the buns. We eat every single biscuit, and we delve into the jellies and everyone has a wobbly bit on his or her plate. Then we cut the enormous cake.

It is simply lovely—but alas, we can't eat it all, it really is too big! Not even Michael, who has the biggest appetite of all, can manage another bit, though he says he wouldn't mind trying if I *really* want all the cake eaten.

Then there are crackers, and we have to pull

those. Pat won't pull hers. She is frightened of the bang, she says!

"Enid Blyton, make your next story about a girl who is scared of pulling crackers!" shouts Robin.

"No! No, don't," says Pat. "I should hate that. You won't, will you?"

"Of course I won't," I say. "Now put on your paper caps, wear your cracker brooches and tie-pins and let's go back into the other room, to see if you want any more stories."

"Yes, we do, we do!" everyone cries, and we rush helter-skelter into the other room. Then we remember we haven't brought our chairs, and back we go for them.

Soon we are all in a ring again. Jennifer and Elizabeth, the twins, pull at my sleeve.

"We haven't had a turn yet. We can have one each, can't we, although we're twins?"

"Of course. I wasn't going to make you share a story," I say. "Well—what do you want?"

The twins stare at each solemnly. "You choose first, Jennifer," says Elizabeth.

"No, you," says Jennifer. They are always nice to one another like that.

"Elizabeth can be first because E comes before J," I say. "Go on, Elizabeth."

"Well—I'd simply love a story about a little house," says Elizabeth. "One you can build. You know, a toy house. We had one once at home, and it had a little roof and a door and windows and everything. You could fit all the parts of the house together—and when we'd done it, the door would open and shut. It was lovely."

"Yes. Do you know a story about a little house like that?" asks Jennifer.

"I do," I say. "It belonged to a small girl called Linda, so we'll call it 'Linda's Little House.' Listen."

Linda's Little House

A Tale for Elizabeth

ON her birthday Linda had an exciting present. She undid the paper, and unwrapped a box. On the front of the box was a picture of a pretty little house, with a green roof, some windows, a green front door, and two red chimneys.

"Oh!" said Linda. "What a darling house!"

She took off the box-lid—and there, inside, were red bricks, green tiles for the roof, little glass windows, a small green front door and two red chimneys.

"You see, it's for you to build," said Mummy. "If you look well at the picture, and copy it, you will see exactly how to build that pretty little house."

So after breakfast Linda sat down on the floor and began to build the new little house.

She built the walls. She slipped the windows

into the spaces she had left in the walls. She put
on the green tiled roof very carefully. She slid the
chimneys into the holes left for them. And last
of all she put in the little front door, which could be
hung on a small hinge and opened and shut
properly. It even had a tiny knocker on it, which
made the smallest rat-tat-tat you ever heard.

"Look, Mummy!" said Linda. "Isn't it lovely?
Now I know how to build a house! Would you
like to see me do it all over again?"

"Yes, I would," said Mummy. So Linda
knocked the tiny house down, and began to build
it all over again. She knocked it down and built
it six times that day. The toys watched her every
time, and thought she was very clever.

That night she left the little house standing by the
toy cupboard when she went to bed. The golliwog
opened the door, bent himself down low and walked
in. The teddy bear was too fat to get inside. The
clockwork mouse ran in, and the small dolls from
the dolls' house. They all thought it was the nicest
house they had ever seen.

"Isn't Linda clever to build it up like that," said
the golly. "She's so quick, too. Really, it doesn't
take her ten minutes to do it!"

Linda often played with the little house. Then
someone gave her a paint-box and she forgot about
the house for a time, and painted pictures instead.

Now one night, when the toys were playing in the
nursery, there came a knocking at the window.

"That's Dance-About the Pixie!" cried the bear

and ran to open the window. It *was* Dance-About
—but a very sad pixie she was. She cried so many
tears on the window-sill that it looked as if it had
been raining there.

"Whatever's the matter?" asked the bear.

"Oh, toys—you know my dear little house in the
woods?" said Dance-About. "The one made out
of that big toadstool? Well, it's gone. A horrid
boy came along this afternoon and kicked it to bits.
It's a good thing I wasn't there, or I'd have been
kicked to bits too. Now I've got no house at all.
There aren't any more toadstools growing. It's
cold without a house—so I've come to ask you what
I ought to do."

The golliwog looked round at the little house
Linda so often built. It was standing by the toy
cupboard. "What about Linda's house?" he said.
I shouldn't think it would matter if you had
that. It is a lovely little house, just big enough
for you, Dance-About."

"So it is," said the pixie, dancing in at the front door, and out again. "But how can I take the house to the woods?"

"It knocks down, and it's quite easy to build up again," said the bear. "Look—this is how you knock it down."

He knocked it all down. Then the toys neatly put the bricks, the tiles, the chimneys and everything into the box, and popped on the lid. The golly and the bear between them carried the box to the woods, and Dance-About showed them where she wanted the house built.

But it wasn't so easy to build as the bear had thought. It was true he had often watched Linda building it, but that wasn't the same as building it himself. He put the chimney where the window ought to be and didn't leave any room for the door. It was a dreadful muddle.

"We'd better go and ask Linda to come and help," said the golliwog at last. "Oh, dear—I hope she won't mind us borrowing the house like this. Bear, go and fetch her, will you?"

So, much to her surprise, Linda was awakened by the bear, who told her what they wanted. She got out of bed at once, excited.

"It was rather naughty of you, bear, to carry my house off like that without even asking me," she said, as she put on her dressing-gown and slippers. "Of course, I'll come—and I'll build the house and let Dance-About have it. Fancy seeing a pixie in the middle of the night like this!"

The bear took her to the place in the woods where the pixie was. All the other toys were there, too, standing round the heap of bricks and tiles on the grass.

Linda began to build the house. The moon shone down and gave her enough light to see by. In ten minutes the house was finished. There it stood in the moonlight, with its red chimneys, shining windows and little front door. It looked so real.

"Oh, thank you!" said Dance-About, skipping in at the door. "It's beautiful. Just the right size, too. I'll get some curtains for the windows to-morrow, and buy some furniture. And I'll give a tea-party when the house is ready to live in. You'll come, won't you, Linda?"

"Of course!" said Linda, joyfully, and off she went back to bed. She could hardly believe it was all true next day when she woke up! But the box was gone, and she was almost sure the bear gave her a smile when she looked at him.

And to-day she found a note tucked under the bear's fat arm. It says:

"Dear Linda,

"My tea-party is at four o'clock to-day. Do come. Tippy-toppy tarts with cream, and Squishy Buns with honey.

"Love from Dance-About."

Linda's going, of course, and she's going to tell me what the Tippy-toppy tarts are, and the Squishy Buns. I hope she brings a few back with her, don't you!

"I'd like that story all over again," says Elizabeth. "And I'd *love* some Tippy-Toppy Tarts and Squishy Buns!"

"So would I," says Peter. "What a pity you didn't have some at tea-time, Enid Blyton."

"I'd have to ask Dance-About how to make them!" I say. "They must be perfectly lovely. Now, Jennifer—your turn. And I'm sure I know what kind of a story you want!"

"*Do* you?" says Jennifer. "What is it then?"

"I'm sure you want one about a horse," I say. I know that both the twins are fond of riding and love horses. Jennifer nods her head.

"Yes, you're right. That's just what I do want. But I'd like some children in it too."

"And a dog," says Elizabeth. "That would be a nice story, with children and a horse and dog in it."

"Is that too difficult for you to think of?" asks Jennifer, anxiously. "I'll take out the dog if you like."

"Oh, no—the dog must go in," I say. "As a matter of fact, it's a puppy. Now, are you ready? I'll tell you the story of 'The Old Black Horse.'"

The Old Black Horse

THERE was once an old black horse who lived by himself in Long Meadow. He was past work and he spent his days pulling at the juicy grass, and remembering his old friends and the good times they had had together.

He was lonely. His friends were far away, still at work for one farmer or another. There were sheep in the next field, but the old horse thought them stupid creatures. There were rabbits in his own field, but they always ran off as soon as they heard his heavy hoofs.

"I wouldn't mind a dog to talk to sometimes," thought the old horse. "I've known some friendly dogs in my time—clever dogs too. But the farmer's two dogs are surly creatures, and never come near me."

At the cottage down the road lived a boy. He was big for his age, and stronger than the other lads. The old horse sometimes saw him passing by the gate, but he always kept out of the way. He didn't want to make friends with that boy!

Tom didn't make friends with anything or any-one! He had quickly found out that he was bigger and stronger than most children of his age, and so he had always got his own way by pushing the others down, or hitting them hard. The other boys and girls were afraid of him, and Tom soon knew that. He liked them to be afraid of him. He liked them to run away when he came along. It made him feel grand and strong and important. He wasn't nice to animals either. He wanted them to be afraid of him too!

And they were. The old horse galloped off to the other end of the field when Tom came by. He knew quite well that Tom could throw stones very hard. It was better to be out of the boy's way! All the cats and dogs ran off when Tom came by, too. He could pull a cat's tail hard, and twist a dog's collar till the poor creature almost choked.

One day the old horse saw, to his great surprise, that Tom had a dog of his own! It was a big, clumsy puppy, with wide brown eyes and a tail that wagged gaily. Someone had given it to the boy, and Tom meant to make it the most obedient dog in the world.

"I've no use for animals who won't do what they are told!" he said to the other boys. "My dog is going to be my slave. When I say 'Come' it will come, and when I say, 'Go' it will go. When I say 'Lie down' it will lie down at once."

That was exactly like Tom. He wasn't going to make a loving friend of his dog—he was going to make it a poor frightened little slave. And he began at once.

The puppy was put on a short lead. He was made to walk close by Tom's legs, almost choking. He was hit when he did not understand an order from Tom. He was scolded the whole time, and never praised or loved.

He soon lost the wag out of his tail, and his ears drooped. He began to be afraid of Tom. He was a dear playful puppy, but as soon as Tom came near he crouched down on the ground and put his tail between his legs.

Tom used to give the puppy his lessons in the lane by the field where the old horse lived. The horse watched through a gap in the hedge. He liked dogs, and he thought the puppy looked a jolly fellow. He felt very sorry for him.

The puppy soon learnt to do what he was told, because he knew that if he didn't he would be struck hard with a stick, or have his collar pulled at so hard that it hurt him. He was taught all sorts of things, but he did them out of fear, not out of love.

One day Tom took the puppy down the lane. He met Harry, Len and Mollie. "Hallo," he said. "See my pup? Like to watch him do some tricks?"

The other children stood and watched. The puppy was told what he was to do. "Now I'm going to throw my stick into this pond, and you are to fetch it," said Tom.

The puppy listened. He looked at the pond. There were ducks on it and he didn't like ducks. They flapped big wings at him. Splash! Tom's stick went into the pond, and he shouted to the puppy.

"Fetch it! Fetch it!"

But the puppy wouldn't. He crouched down on the ground and shivered. The other children laughed. Tom was very angry.

"What! You won't obey me, you tiresome little thing!" he yelled. "You shall have a beating."

He struck the puppy with a stick and the dog howled in pain.

"Don't," said Mollie. "You're cruel."

"Stop," said Harry. "He's only a pup."

"I'll beat you too, if you give me orders about my own dog!" said Tom, angrily. The puppy howled again.

The old horse had been watching. He was afraid of Tom, too—but he couldn't bear to hear the dog whining so pitifully. He suddenly jumped over the hedge, and landed near the children with a crash.

They all jumped, and the puppy fled behind a bush in fear.

The horse cantered up to Tom. He put his big head behind the boy's back and caught hold of his belt with his teeth. Tom felt himself suddenly jerked off his feet. Holding him tightly, though the boy was struggling hard, the old horse trotted a little way down the lane to where a big holly bush stood. The horse knew how prickly it was, for he had pricked his nose on it many times. With a jerk of his strong head he threw the boy straight into the middle of the bush!

"Ow-yow-ow!" yelled Tom, as the prickles stuck into him. "Ow-yow-ow! You horrid thing! Get me out, Harry, quick"!

But Harry didn't. He stood and laughed. So did the others. "It serves you right," said Harry. "I'm not a bit sorry for you, Tom. You are always using your strength to hurt others weaker or smaller than yourself—and now someone stronger than you is using his strength to punish *you*. Ha, ha!"

Tom wriggled out of the bush, yelling with pain and anger. He fell to the ground, jumped up, and rushed at Harry to hit him. But the old horse stepped in again, caught hold of Tom, and this time swung him right over and into the duck-pond. There was a frightened scurrying of ducks—and splash! Tom was in the muddy water. He came up gasping and spluttering, to see the other children screaming with laughter.

"Good old horse! It serves you right, Tom!"

The farmer came up, grinning, as Tom waded out of the pond, wet and muddy. He laid his hand on the old horse's neck.

"The old horse has done what I've longed to do many a time, my lad!" he said. "Let it be a lesson to you. You're a bully—and my old horse has bullied you, so that you know now what it's like. Not very pleasant, is it? I've watched you bullying that pup of yours—and the other children, too. You go home and get dry—and make up your mind in the future that you will be a friend to others, and not an enemy."

Tom went off, crying. The children ran home. The farmer put the horse back into the field, giving him a pat on his long nose. The puppy squeezed through a gap in the hedge and ran to the old horse's shaggy feet.

"Thank you," he wuffed. "You saved me from a beating. Perhaps Tom will be nicer now."

"Maybe," neighed the old horse. "And maybe not. But you just come and tell me when he's not, and I'll deal with him again. We'll be friends, you and I."

"We will!" yelped the puppy in delight, and galloped round and about the old horse. "Come on—let's have a race. I like you. You're the nicest horse I've ever met."

And now the two are great friends, and the old horse isn't lonely any more. Tom knows quite well that his puppy tells the old horse everything, and he is very careful to be kind to him instead of cruel. He doesn't want to be thrown into the pond again! It was a good thing for everyone that the old black horse was sensible enough that summer's day to put matters right himself, wasn't it!

"Good old black horse!" says Jennifer. "I'm jolly glad he did that to Tom. I'd have done it too if I'd been a horse. That was a good story, and I liked it."

"I like when people get punished for horrid things they do," says Robin. "Can't we have a story about another naughty boy? I do like those."

"You've had your turn, Robin," says Mollie, at once. "Hasn't he, Enid Blyton? He can't choose twice."

"I'm not going to," says Robin, looking hurt. "I was only just saying I *like* those stories."

"*I'd* like a story now," says Kenneth. "I've waited and waited for my turn. Can I have *my* story now?"

"Yes, you can," I say. "What do you want your story to be about?"

"Well, I've got a teddy bear at home," says Kenneth. "And he always looks grumpy. *Really* grumpy, you know, and I'm sure he's always grumbling about things to the other toys. Do you know a story about a grumpy teddy bear?"

"Yes, I do," I say. "It's quite a funny one, too. Would a funny one do for you, Kenneth?"

"I'd like that very much," says Kenneth. "Right," I say. "I'll tell you the story of 'The Teddy Bear's Tail.'"

The TEDDY BEAR'S TAIL

A Tale for Kenneth

THE teddy bear was really tiresome. He was such a grumbler, and every day he seemed to find something new to complain about.

"I wish I could bounce," he said, when he saw how well the ball could bounce. "I do wish I could. I would bounce right up to the mantelpiece then, and see if I could take a sweet out of the tin there."

Then another time he said : "I do wish I had a key. The train has a key, and the clockwork mouse, and so has the clown. But I haven't. It isn't fair."

When he saw the dolls sitting in a row, all beautifully dressed, he had another fine grumble.

"Look at those dolls!" he said. "All with hats and coats and dresses and shoes! And I haven't any clothes at all. Not even a ribbon round my neck. It isn't fair. I've only got my skin."

"You've got a nice *furry* skin," said the pink cat. "Don't grumble so."

Then the teddy found something else to grumble about. He looked behind himself for the first time and saw that he hadn't got a tail! He stared in surprise.

" Where's my tail?" he said.

"You never had one," said the black dog.

"Why not?" asked the bear. "I'm an animal, aren't I? Then why haven't I a tail?"

"How should I know?" said the toy dog. He wagged his own black tail, looking pleased with it.

"I've got a tail too," squeaked the clockwork mouse.

"So have I," said the pink cat, and she swung it round to show the bear.

"Mine's the longest," said the toy monkey, and flapped it in the bear's face.

"Don't," said the bear, crossly. "Oh, I do think it's terribly unfair. *Why* haven't I got a tail? Have I lost it?"

"I told you. You never had one," said the dog, and he gave a giggle.

Well, after that the bear was dreadfully tiresome. He went on and on grumbling because he hadn't got a tail. At last the golliwog could bear it no longer.

One night, when the bear had gone out on to

the landing outside the nursery door, he spoke to
the toys. "For goodness' sake, let's give the bear
some sort of a tail. I shall go mad if I hear him
wail because he's no tail."

"Why does the teddy bear wail? Because he
hasn't a tail," said the pink cat at once, feeling
clever. "That rhymes."

"Be quiet," said the golliwog, wishing he had
made up the rhyme himself. "Now—who will give
the bear his tail? Clockwork mouse, will you?"

"No," said the mouse. "I want mine."

"Will you, black dog?" asked the golly. "You've
had yours for ages."

"And I want it for ages more," said the dog.
"I keep my wag in it."

Nobody would give up their tail. It was very
annoying. But at last the old kite in the toy cupboard spoke in his funny, windy voice.

"He can have *my* tail. I'm broken now. I
shan't fly any more, and as I only use my tail when
I fly, it's no use to me now."

"Well—it's rather a funny tail," said the golliwog,
doubtfully. "I don't know if it will suit a bear."

"Don't ask him if it will suit him," said the kite.
"Just give it to him. Tie it on him when he's asleep.
He's always grumbling because he hasn't got one,
isn't he? Well, make him have one, and tell him
to stop grumbling."

The toys giggled. They thought they would do
that. It amused them to think of the teddy bear
running about the nursery with an enormously

long tail made of paper twists tied on to string! That was what the kite's tail was made of!

So, the next time the bear sat in a corner of the toy cupboard to go to sleep, the golliwog snipped off the kite's tail, and neatly tied it on to the back of the teddy bear. He did it so gently that the bear didn't know it. He just lay there, fast asleep.

He woke up very soon, and stood up. He thought he would go and have a run round the nursery with the clockwork mouse, who was busy running all round the hearth-rug. The golliwog had wound him up, and he was having a fine time.

So the bear stepped out of the toy cupboard and began to run to the mouse. Rustle-rustle-rustle went something behind him, and he jumped in fright. He turned round quickly and saw, to his horror, that he had a long, long tail unwinding itself over the carpet.

"What is it?" he yelled.

"Your new tail," said the golly, with a grin. "You are always grumbling because you haven't got one, and we were so tired of hearing you—so the kite has given you his tail to wear."

"I don't like it," said the bear. "Take it off!"

"What! After we have gone to all the trouble of

putting it on you for a lovely surprise!" cried the pink cat. "Ungrateful creature! Certainly we shan't take it off!"

The bear hated his new tail. For one thing it made such a rustly noise behind him. For another thing, it was so very long, and kept getting caught round table-legs and things like that, so that the bear spent half his time untangling it. Sometimes it tangled itself round his legs and made him fall over. He got very, very angry with it.

And then one day Donald, the little boy in whose nursery the toys lived, picked up his teddy, and was most astonished to see the long, long tail tied to him. He took it off at once.

"You've got all tangled up with the kite's tail!" he said. "There—now you're all right."

The bear was delighted. How lovely it was to run about the nursery at night again without having a horrid long tail rustling behind him and getting caught round everything. The toys looked at one another and smiled.

"Poor bear — sorry you've lost your tail," said the golliwog. "We'll get you another. A tale out of a book, perhaps."

"I don't want a tail," said the bear.

"Well, be careful you don't grumble again

because you haven't something that other people have got," said the golliwog. "If you grumble because you've no whiskers we'll give you enormous ones made of the hairs from the mane of the rocking-horse!"

"And if you grumble because you've no key, we'll make a hole and fit the key of the clock there," giggled the pink cat. "Then you'll say tick-tock whenever we wind you up."

"And if you grumble because you haven't any clothes to wear, we will dress you up like a baby doll and see how funny you look," laughed the curly-haired doll.

"I shan't grumble any more," said the bear, in rather a small voice. And he didn't. He was quite a nice bear after that—but there was one toy he would never, never speak to, and that was the old kite in the cupboard.

But you may be sure the kite didn't mind that!

"Well, that's *just* the kind of tale I like," says Kenneth. "And it's just the kind my teddy *won't* like, if I tell it to him—but I really think I must!"

"I shall tell it to my little sister," says Peter. "She'll love it. She's got a teddy bear too—but he's a nice smiley one. Is it my turn yet, Enid Blyton?"

"Yes—you can choose now," I say, because Peter really has been very patient indeed. "What kind of story do you want, Peter?"

"I'd like a story about a naughty boy," says Peter. "I like stories like that."

"Very well—but what kind of a naughty boy?" I ask. "A greedy one? An untruthful one? A cheeky one?"

"Oh, yes—a rude, cheeky boy," says Peter. "Make him *very* rude, and tell us what happened to him."

"Well, I'll tell you the story of Timothy, then," I say, "the boy who was always rude to his mother and father, and to his teachers too. It's called 'The Cheeky Boy.'"

THE CHEEKY BOY

A Tale for Peter

THERE was once a little boy who loved to be cheeky. He spoke rudely to his mother and father, and he was cheeky even to his teacher.

He thought it was clever! It made him feel rather grand to say rude things. The other children stared at him when he said, "Shan't!" or "Won't," and when he put his tongue out behind his mother's back, he felt quite a hero. The other children laughed at him sometimes, but they thought he was rather horrid, all the same.

He thought it was funny to interrupt the grown-ups when they were talking. He kept pulling his mother's arm, and pretending to want something when she was speaking to her friends. He answered cheekily when they asked him polite questions.

96

"How are you, Timothy?" they would say. "Do you like school?"

"No, I hate it," Timothy would answer, which was not at all true. But he thought it was clever to say cheeky things like that. He would contradict people too, and that made his mother cross.

"It's very warm to-day," she would say. And Timothy would answer at once : "It isn't. It's cold as ice!"

"I wish you wouldn't be so cheeky," his mother would sigh. "It's so unpleasant."

Of course, what he wanted was a good spanking, but nobody gave him that, which was a great pity, because in the end he got a much bigger punishment.

It all happened one night. Timmy woke up suddenly, and heard the clock strike twelve. And at that very same moment he saw what looked like a brownie in his bedroom. It was most astonishing. The boy sat up at once.

"Hallo," said the brownie. "I've lost my way, somehow. Is this your bedroom?"

"Oh no, it's the kitchen!" said Timothy, in his usual cheeky manner. "Who are you?"

"I'm a brownie," said the little fellow.

"Fibber!" said Timothy. "There aren't any brownies, or fairies, or elves. I know that. Now you just hop off, funny-face!"

The brownie stared at him sternly. "Have you no manners, boy?" he asked.

G

"Plenty," said Timmy. "Do you want to buy some?"

"Don't be cheeky," said the brownie, in disgust.

"Would you rather I was nosey?" said Timothy, in his cheekiest voice.

"My word—you must be Timothy, the cheeky boy!" said the brownie, suddenly. "I've heard people talk about you, and say what a pity it is you haven't been brought up better! No—I don't want you to be nosey. You can be cheeky. Yes—you can be CHEEKY—CHEEKY —CHEEKY!"

And as he spoke, he vanished in a most peculiar way, just as smoke grows thinner and vanishes. Timmy could just hear his voice saying "CHEEKY" over and over again, and then it stopped, and there was nobody and nothing there.

"A dream!" thought Timothy. "A silly dream. But wasn't I smart in it? My word, I do feel sharp when I'm cheeky."

"You'll do as you're told," he said. "I'll make you up some medicine to take, which will, I'm afraid, be very nasty. And I'll give you some lotion to bathe your cheeks with. It will smart, but that can't be helped."

So there was poor Timmy, put to bed on the day of a party, drinking horrible medicine and having his cheeks bathed with a lotion that smarted like stinging-nettles. He felt very sorry indeed for himself and he cried when he was alone. All that day he lay there, seeing nobody, hearing the children go to the party next door. He took his nasty medicine every hour, and had his cheeks bathed every two hours. He looked at himself in the glass, and was filled with horror when he saw how ugly he looked.

"Mother, will I always look as ugly as this?" asked poor Timmy.

"You'll look all right as soon as your cheeks go down," said his mother, looking worried and anxious. "Now, see if you can go to sleep for a bit."

But Timmy couldn't. He lay and listened to the shouts of laughter from next door, and he heard the popping of crackers. Then, after two or three hours, he heard the children going home. And suddenly he got a fright!

Someone was looking in at his window! It was Harry! He had been to the party next door, and had suddenly thought he would like to have a word with poor Timmy. He had climbed up the old apple tree outside the boy's bedroom, and there he was, grinning through the window.

"Hallo," said Timmy, hardly able to speak now because his cheeks were so big.

"Timmy! What's the matter with you!" cried Harry, and the grin faded from his face. "You look simply terrible, I've never seen anyone so ugly in my life."

"It's awful," said Timmy. "I don't know what happened to make me like this. I'm all cheeks."

"Well," said Harry, his grin coming back again, suddenly, "well—we always knew you were a cheeky boy—and now you certainly are the most CHEEKY person I've ever seen—yes, all cheeks. Perhaps it's because you always were cheeky that you've gone like that!"

A voice called out sternly from below the window. "Harry! Come down at once. You know you've got your best suit on."

Harry disappeared suddenly. He didn't dare to be cheeky to *his* mother. He respected her too much. Timmy was left alone, thinking hard.

He remembered the funny dream he had had the night before—when he thought he had seen a brownie. Perhaps it *wasn't* a dream! Perhaps it had been real. Perhaps—perhaps—that little

fellow had put a sort of spell on him. Timmy
remembered his voice, saying : "You can be
CHEEKY—CHEEKY—CHEEKY!"

"He'll come again to-night to see what has
happened," thought Timothy. "I'll ask him to
make me right again. I can't go on like this—
everyone thinking I'm ill, and not coming near me."

But the brownie didn't come! Timothy never
saw him again. So the next day his cheeks were
still swollen and he still had to take the medicine
and have his face bathed.

He had a lot of time to think. He began to
notice that every time he was rude or cheeky, his
cheeks swelled up a little more—but if he answered
politely and kindly, they seemed to go down.

"I suppose that the only person who can cure me
is myself," thought Timothy, at last. "Well, I
shall miss school and games and miss going to the
circus and going out to tea if I don't do something
about it. I shall have to stop being cheeky. It's
a pity, because it made
me feel so smart. But
I can't have cheek
going to my cheeks!"

He began to be polite
in his answers. He
didn't contradict. He
didn't answer back. He
didn't interrupt others,
and bit by bit his
balloon-like cheeks

went down, until one day he looked quite himself again. The doctor came to see him and smiled.

"Ah—he's all right again now. He can go back to school. A most peculiar illness. I can't think what it was, even now!"

"It seems to have done him good, doctor," said Timmy's mother. "He's so quiet and polite now— quite a different boy. Not at all cheeky."

The doctor laughed. "You're right—he's certainly not CHEEKY any more. Let's hope he won't be either."

Well, the last time I saw Timothy, he had one cheek just a little bit swollen, but he was hoping nobody would notice. It was harder to get out of the habit of being cheeky than he had thought! Poor Timothy. He had a dreadful time, hadn't he, but if it taught him to be polite and well-mannered, it was worth it.

"I guess Timothy wasn't cheeky any more!" says Peter. "Oh, I *do* wish I could have seen him when he was all cheeks. I thought that was a lovely story. I wish it had been longer."

"We've only got three more stories," says Daisy. "Oh, dear—it sounded so lovely to have fourteen—but the time just rushes by when we're listening. Can I have *my* story now, please, Enid Blyton? I know just what I want."

"What do you want, Daisy?" I say.

"I'd like a story about a pixie and a little girl and some magic," says Daisy. "A really nice one, please."

They all look at me and wait. A pixie—a little girl—and some magic. Yes—I know a story with all those in!

"I know just the story for you, Daisy," I say. "And what is more—it's got daisies in, so it's just exactly right for a little girl called Daisy— which is you!"

"I shall like that," says Daisy, and she pulls her chair as close as she can. "Do begin."

"It's about a pixie and a little girl called Linda," I say. "And it's called 'Pink Paint for a Pixie.'"

Pink Paint for a Pixie

A Tale for Daisy

ONCE, when Linda was playing at the bottom of her garden, she heard a funny noise. She stopped and listened.

"If a bird could speak, it would speak just like that funny voice," thought Linda, in surprise. "It *is* somebody talking—it's a very small voice, high and clear."

She sat perfectly still, listening, trying to hear what the voice said.

"Just my luck!" said the voice. "Finished the tea-set all but three cups—and now I've run out of paint. Isn't that just my luck?"

Linda quietly popped her head through a gap in the hedge to see who could be talking. It didn't at all sound like a child. It wasn't a child, either.

"It's a pixie!" said Linda, in the greatest surprise. "Well, who would have thought I'd ever see a pixie! I've looked for years and years and never seen one. But this *must* be one—and he's talking to himself. What is he doing?"

She looked closely and saw that he was painting a very small tea-set, just big enough for himself to drink from. The cups and saucers were about the size of the ones in Linda's doll's house.

Suddenly the tiny fellow heard Linda breathing

and he looked up. He stared in surprise at the little girl's head peeping through the hedge.

"Hullo!" he said. "Isn't it a nuisance—I've run out of pink paint."

"What are you doing?" asked Linda.

"I'm painting a pretty pattern on these cups," said the pixie, and he held one up for Linda to see.

He certainly was putting a very pretty pattern on each one. There were pink roses, and green leaves all the way round. The saucers and plates had the same pattern.

Linda looked at the tiny tubes of paint beside the pixie. The tube of pink paint was squeezed quite empty.

"Can't you finish your work?" she asked.

"No," said the pixie. "And I promised the Princess Peronel she should have the whole set to-morrow, for her birthday party. It's really annoying."

Linda suddenly had a splendid idea. *She* had some tubes of paint in her paint-box. One might be pink. If so, she could lend it to the pixie!

"I believe I could help you," she said. "I've got some paints. I'll go and get the tube of pink. Wait here a minute."

She ran indoors and found her paint-box. "Darling, surely you are not going to paint indoors this fine morning!" said her mother, when she saw Linda getting out her paint-box.

"No, Mummy—I'm lending a tube of pink paint to a pixie," said Linda.

Her mother laughed. "What funny things you do say, Linda!" she said. She didn't guess for a minute that Linda was speaking the truth. She thought she was just pretending.

Linda ran out again, holding in her hand a tube of crimson paint. She knew that if the pixie mixed the deep red with water, the colour would be pink. She was soon back at the hedge again.

"Here you are," she said. "I'm sure this will make a lovely pink."

"You *are* a good friend!" said the pixie, gratefully. "You can watch me paint if you like."

Linda sat and watched him. He had a tiny china palette on which he mixed his colours. He squeezed some of the crimson out on to it, and then dipped his tiny brush into a dewdrop hanging on a grass nearby. Soon he had just the right pink for the little cups. It was fun to watch him painting roses round the cup he was holding.

"I don't know what I should have done if you hadn't helped me," he said. "Can I do anything for you in return?"

"I suppose you couldn't make a wish come true, could you?" asked Linda, at once. The pixie shook his head.

"No," he said. "I don't know powerful enough magic for that. If I did I'd have wished for a new tube of pink paint for myself. But if you really want a wish to come true why don't you find a four-leaved clover, put it under your pillow, and wish before you go to sleep?"

"There aren't any four-leaved clovers round about here," said Linda. "I and the other children have looked and looked, but we have never found one."

"Well, go to where the foxgloves grow, pick up a fallen foxglove bell, slip it on your thumb and wish," said the pixie.

"The foxgloves aren't out yet," said Linda.

"Of course they aren't!" said the pixie. "How silly of me. Well, try the pink-tipped daisy spell, then."

"What's that?" asked Linda.

"You pick thirteen pink-tipped daisies," said the pixie. "You make them into a daisy-chain, and wear them round your neck for one hour, at four o'clock in the daytime. You wish your wish thirteen times in that hour. Then you take off the chain and put the daisies in water. You mustn't forget to do that, because if you don't give them a drink, the magic won't work."

"That sounds a good spell," said Linda. "But there aren't any pink-tipped daisies round here, pixie. Look—they are quite white."

The little girl picked two or three daisies and showed them to the pixie. He looked underneath the petals at the very tips. He shook his head.

"You're right," he said. "Not a pink tip to be

seen. Very tiresome. Well, I must think of something else for you."

A bell rang in the distance. Linda got up. "That's for my dinner," she said. "I must go. I'll come back again afterwards."

"I'll think of something whilst you are

gone," said the pixie. He
thought and he thought.
But he could think of no
other way of making a
wish come true. He was
only a small pixie, not
very old, and he really
didn't know a great deal
of magic.

Then a fine idea came
into his small head. Hadn't he got plenty of pink
paint in that tube? Well, why shouldn't he paint
all the daisies round about with pink tips?

"Good idea!" he said, and as soon as he finished
his tea-set, he went to the daisies, sat underneath
the little flowers, and carefully ran his brush, full
of pink paint, under the tip of each petal. Soon
the first daisy looked really pretty. It turned up
its petals a little to show the pink underneath.

"I hope Linda comes back soon," thought the
pixie. "Then I can tell her what I've done."

But Linda didn't come back. Her mother had
said she must have a rest after dinner, and the little
girl was on her bed, hoping that the pixie would
still be in the field when she got up at three o'clock.

He wasn't. He had packed up his painted tea-set for the Princess Peronel and had gone. But there were the daisies, all pink-tipped! And there was the little tube of paint left beside them, half-empty now, with the top put neatly on.

Linda looked round for the pixie, when she crept out through the hedge into the field after her rest. He wasn't there. But there was her tube of paint—and, oh, what a surprise, it was lying by a daisy-plant, where four pink-tipped daisies grew together, their golden eyes looking straight at Linda!

"He's painted your tips pink! The underneath of your pretty white petals is crimson pink! Now I can try that magic spell!"

Linda picked thirteen daisies and made them into a chain. You know how she made it, don't you? She slit each stalk near its end with a pin, and then slipped a daisy through the slit, so that soon the thirteen were hanging in a pretty chain. She joined the chain—and looked at her watch.

"Four o'clock! Now I'll wear it—and for one hour I will wish my wish thirteen times!"

She wore the daisy-chain, and wished her wish thirteen times in the hour. Then she took off the chain and put the daisies into water to have a drink. She wished for her big soldier-brother to come back from far away—and, will you believe it, he came home the very next day. She rushed out to tell the pixie, but she has never seen him again.

Have you seen pink-tipped daisies? Go out and look for some ; maybe you will find thirteen!

"Oh—*can* we go out and look for some pink-tipped daisies this very minute!" cries Daisy, as soon as I have finished the story. "Do let's! Oh, I'd so love to find some and make a daisy-chain, and wish thirteen times!"

"No—don't let's go yet," says Jack. "I haven't had *my* story—and it will soon be time to go home! We can look for daisies when we have to go."

"Yes, you can," I say. "I'm afraid I shall soon have to send you all home, and certainly Jack mustn't miss his story! What would you like, Jack?"

"Well, I've just had a bicycle for my birthday," says Jack. "It's a beauty. But I'm not allowed to ride it in the street till I've learnt Safety First rules—the Highway Code, it's called. Do you know a story about a boy who's just got a new bicycle?"

"Yes, I do," I say. "And it's about a boy called Peter—who *didn't* learn the rules of Safety First! It's called 'Peter's Birthday.'"

Peter's Birthday

A Tale for Jack

PETER woke up on his birthday and saw the sun shining brightly in at his window. He sat up joyfully.

"Proper birthday weather. I'm nine to-day—and Dad always promised me a bicycle when I was nine. I do wonder if he has remembered."

He dressed and went downstairs—and the very first thing he saw, glittering and shining outside on the verandah, was a brand new bicycle! Peter rushed

to it in delight, shouting at the top of his voice.
"Dad, you remembered! Oh, what a beauty!"

"Happy birthday, Peter," said his father and
mother, both together. Then his father stopped
him from getting on his bicycle to ride round the
garden.

"Now wait a moment. Before you even get on
that bicycle, you've got to read every bit of what the
Highway Code says about bicyclists! Every word
—and you've got to remember it too!"

Peter looked sulky. "Oh blow! What's the
sense of that? I've learnt to ride already, and I
know all about the traffic lights, and putting my
hand out to go round corners and things like that."

"And before you go for your first ride *I* want to
say a few things," said his mother. "You're so
hasty and careless, Peter, and I want to be quite
sure you know everything you ought to know before
you go riding."

"Oh, Mother—don't lecture me on my birthday," groaned Peter. "It's going to be such a nice
day with cards and presents—and my party this
afternoon, with a birthday cake and ices! Balloons
and crackers! Smashing!"

His mother laughed. "I'm not lecturing you,
you silly boy. it's a mother's duty to tell her
children the rules of the road when they first have a
bicycle. Well, I'll tell you after breakfast. Come
along now, and see your cards and other presents.
You can read the Highway Code before you go out."

Well, after breakfast the telephone bell rang and

his mother went to answer it. His father was going round the garden with the gardener. Peter stood impatiently in the hall, wishing he could go for his first ride.

"I'll just get on my bike and ride down the road and back," he thought, getting tired of waiting. "I can't possibly come to any harm! I've ridden round Ned's garden hundreds of times, and I shall be quite safe on the road."

So he jumped on his bicycle, rode round the garden path, and out of the gate, feeling very happy. His own bright, shining bike! It was wonderful. He rang the bell loudly to tell a dog to get out of the way. He put his hand out to show everyone he was about to go round the corner. He stopped at the traffic lights because they showed red.

It was fun to be out on the road with motors and lorries all about. Better than riding round and round a garden! Peter began pedalling up the steep hill outside the town. He puffed and panted, and then he saw, just in front of him, a lorry going steadily up the hill. Peter pedalled hard to catch it up and then caught hold of the back of the lorry. "You can jolly well pull me up the hill!" he said to the lorry, and up he went behind it, not pedalling at all.

The lorry got to the top and came to the level again. Peter still held on, enjoying being towed along. And then things happened all at once, as accidents always do!

A dog ran in front of the lorry. The driver pulled up with a jerk. Peter's bicycle ran straight into the back of the lorry, and he fell off. A car behind didn't pull up in time and ran into the back of the lorry too. Poor Peter and his bicycle were between the car and the lorry.

What a to-do there was! The dog barked. The lorry-driver got down at once. The driver of the car leapt out. Peter was pulled out of the mess, with bits of broken bicycle sticking to him!

"Why, it's little Peter Brown!" said a woman. "I'll go and telephone to his mother! Dear, dear— what a silly boy to hang on to the back of a lorry like that. I'm surprised his father and mother didn't tell him the rules of the road!"

Poor Peter! His leg was broken and he had to spend his birthday in hospital. His bicycle was smashed to bits— his lovely new bicycle! He couldn't eat any birthday cake or pull any crackers.

"It's a dreadful price to pay for a minute's foolishness," said his father, "and a terrible way to learn to be careful!"

So it was. I'd rather read the Highway Code and listen to a bit of sound advice, than learn by smashing up my bicycle and my leg, wouldn't you?"

"I shall learn the Safety First rules to-morrow morning," says Jack, as soon as I finish the story. "I couldn't bear to have an accident like that. There was only one thing wrong with my story, Enid Blyton!"

"What was that?" I ask.

"It was too short!" says Peter. I would have liked a long, long one."

"We've had thirteen stories," says Pat. "Oh, dear—only one more. Whose turn is it now?" Well, do you know whose turn it is? It's *your* turn, because you are really supposed to be at my story-party too! You're the very last one to choose. What story will you have?

What? You don't mind a bit? Well, perhaps you would like a Christmassy one? We haven't had one like that, have we? I'll tell you the tale of 'The Man Who Wasn' Father Christmas!'"

The Man who

wasn't
Father Christmas

A Tale for You

THERE was once an old man with a long white beard who loved children. He was very poor, so he couldn't give the children anything, and you can guess that he always wished at Christmas-time that he was Father Christmas.

"Goodness! What fun I'd have if I were Father Christmas!" he thought. "Think of having a sack that was always full of toys—that couldn't be emptied, because it was magic. How happy I should be!"

Now one Christmas-time the old man saw a little notice in the window of a big shop. This is what it said:

"WANTED. A man with a white beard to be Father Christmas, and give out paper leaflets in the street."

Well, the old man stared at this notice, and

wondered if he could get the job. How lovely to dress up as Father Christmas, and go up and down the streets with all the children staring at him! He would be so happy.

So he marched into the shop and asked if he could have the job.

"The work is not hard," said the shopman. "All you have to do is to dress up in a red cloak and trousers and big boots, and take a sack with you."

"Will it be full of toys?" asked the old man, his eyes shining at the thought.

"Of course not!" said the shopman. "It will be full of leaflets for you to give to the passers-by. I have had these leaflets printed to tell everyone to come to our shop this Christmas and buy their presents here. I thought it would be a good idea to dress somebody up as Father Christmas, and let him give out the leaflets."

"I see," said the old man. "I rather thought it would be nice to give the children something."

"Well, what an idea!" said the shopman. "Now, see if this red Father Christmas costume fits you."

It fitted the old man well. He got into it and looked at himself in the glass. He really looked exactly like old Father Christmas. His long white beard flowed down over his chest and his bright blue eyes twinkled brightly.

He took his sack of leaflets and went out. It was the day before Christmas and everyone was busy shopping. How the children stared when they saw the old man walking along in the road!

"It's Father Christmas!" they shouted. "It's Father Christmas! Come and see him!"

Soon the children were crowding round the old man, asking if they could peep into his sack. But alas, there were no toys there, and all he had to give the children were the leaflets. The children were disappointed.

"Fancy Father Christmas only giving us leaflets about Mr. White's shop," they said. "We thought he was a kind old man—but he isn't. He didn't even give us a sweet."

The old man heard the children saying these things and he was sad. "I made a mistake in taking this job," he said to himself. "It is horrid to pretend to be somebody kind and not to be able

to give the boys and girls even a penny! I feel dreadful!"

It began to snow. The old man plodded along the streets, giving out his leaflets. And suddenly he heard a curious sound. It was the sound of bells!

"Where are those bells, I wonder?" thought the old man, looking all round. "It sounds like horse-bells. But everyone has cars

nowadays. There are
no horses in this town."

It wasn't horse-bells
he heard. It was rein-
deer-bells! To the
great surprise of the
old man, a large sleigh
drove down the road,
drawn by reindeer.
And in it was—well,
you can guess without
being told—the *real*
Father Christmas!

The sleigh drew up,
and Father Christmas
leaned out. "Am I
anywhere near the town of Up-and-Down?" he
called. Then he stared hard at the old man—
and he frowned.

"You look like *me!*" he said. "Why are you
dressed like that?"

"Well, just to get a job of work," said the old
man. "But really because I love children, and I
thought if I dressed up like you, they would think I
was you, and would come round me and be happy.
But all I have in my sack is stupid leaflets about
somebody's shop—I haven't any toys to give away,
as you have. So instead of making the children
happy I have disappointed them. I am sorry now
I ever took this job."

"Well, well, you did it for the best," said Father

Christmas, smiling suddenly. "I like people who love children. They are always the nicest people, you know. Look here—would you like to do me a good turn?"

"I'd love to," said the old man.

"Well," said Father Christmas, "I haven't had any tea, and I feel so hungry and thirsty. Would you mind taking care of my reindeer for me whilst I'm in a tea-shop? They don't like standing still, so you'll have to drive them round and round the town. And if you meet any children, you must do exactly as I always do."

"What's that?" asked the old man, his eyes shining.

"You must stop, and say to them, 'A happy Christmas to you! What would you like out of my sack?' And you must let the child dip its hand into my sack and take out what it wants. You won't mind doing that, will you? I always do that as I drive along."

"*Mind* doing that! It would be the thing I would like best in the world," said the old man, hardly believing his ears. "It's—it's—it's—well, I just can't tell you how happy it will make me. I can't believe it's true!"

Father Christmas smiled his wide smile. He jumped down from the sleigh and threw the reins to the old man.

"Come back in an hour," he said. "I'll have finished my tea by then."

He went into a tea-shop. The old man climbed into the driving-seat. He was trembling with joy. He looked at the enormous sack beside him on the seat. It was simply bursting with toys! He cracked the whip and the reindeer set off with a jingling of bells.

Soon they met three children. How those children stared! Then they went quite mad with delight and yelled to the old man : "Father Christmas! Father Christmas! Stop a minute, do!"

The old man stopped the reindeer. He beamed at the children. "A happy Christmas to you!" he said. "What would you like out of my sack?"

"An engine, please," said the boy.

"A doll, please," said one of the girls.

"A book, please," said another girl.

"Dip into my sack and find what you want," said the old man. And with shining faces the three children dipped in their hands . . . and each of them pulled out exactly what he wanted! They rushed home with shouts of joy.

Well, the old man stopped at every child he met, wished them a happy Christmas, and asked them what they wanted. And dozens of happy children dipped into the enormous sack and pulled out just what they longed for.

At the end of an hour the old man drove the reindeer back to the tea-shop. Father Christmas was waiting, putting on his big fur gloves. He smiled when he saw the bright face of the old man.

"You've had a good time, I can see," he said. "Thanks so much. I don't give presents to grown-ups usually—but you might hang up your stocking just for fun to-night. Good-bye!"

He drove off with a ringing of sleigh-bells. The old man went back to the shop in a happy dream, took off his red clothes and went home.

"I've never been so happy before," he said as he got into bed. "Never! If only people knew how wonderful it is to give happiness to others! How lucky Father Christmas is to go about the world giving presents to all the boys and girls!"

The old man hung up his stocking, though he felt rather ashamed of it. And when he woke up in the morning, what do you think was in it?

A magic purse was in it—a purse that was always full of pennies! No matter how many were taken out, there were always some left.

"A penny-purse—a magic penny-purse!" cried the old man joyfully. "My word—what fun I'll have with the children now!"

He does—for he always has a penny to give each one. I wonder if you've ever seen the little penny-purse. It is black and has two letters in silver on the front. They are "F.C." I expect you can guess what they stand for!

"I really think I liked that story best of all," says Michael.

"So did I," says Susan. "It was just right! I did like that old man who wasn't really Father Christmas."

I hope *you* liked your story too. I tried to think of a specially nice one for you. And now the clock strikes half-past six, and it's time for everyone to go home.

"What a pity!" says Jack, fetching in the coats and hats with Peter and Joan to help him. "I could have listened to at least twenty more stories. Enid Blyton, will you give another story-party please—or a story-picnic, perhaps? That would be lovely."

"Well, I might," I say, helping them all on with their hats and coats. "I've enjoyed this party too, though I think my voice is getting rather hoarse. Still, I don't expect any of you mind *that!*"

"Thank you for a lovely time," says Susan, politely.

"Thank you for your nice story-party," says Pat.

"And thank you, thank you for so many stories!" cried Joan. "You'll think of lots more, won't you! Promise you will!"

"I promise!" I say, and take you all to the door. Down the path you go, helter-skelter—and *you* are the last of all. I wave to you—and I can just see your hand waving to me over the wall, and hear your voice, calling good-bye.

Good-bye, all of you, good-bye—till our next exciting story-party! You'll be sure to come, won't you?